# Jellyfish

Written by Jo Windsor

Rigby

Look at the jellyfish.
Jellyfish look like jelly.

Jellyfish can be little.
Jellyfish can be big.

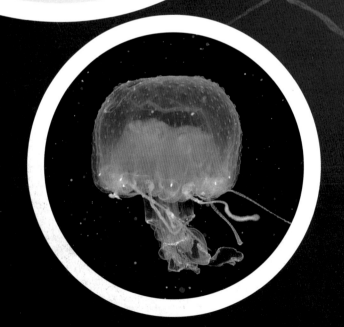

3

Look at the jellyfish.

Jellyfish can be red.
Jellyfish can be blue.

Jellyfish can be pink,
too.

a blue jellyfish

a pink jellyfish

5

Jellyfish can look
like umbrellas.

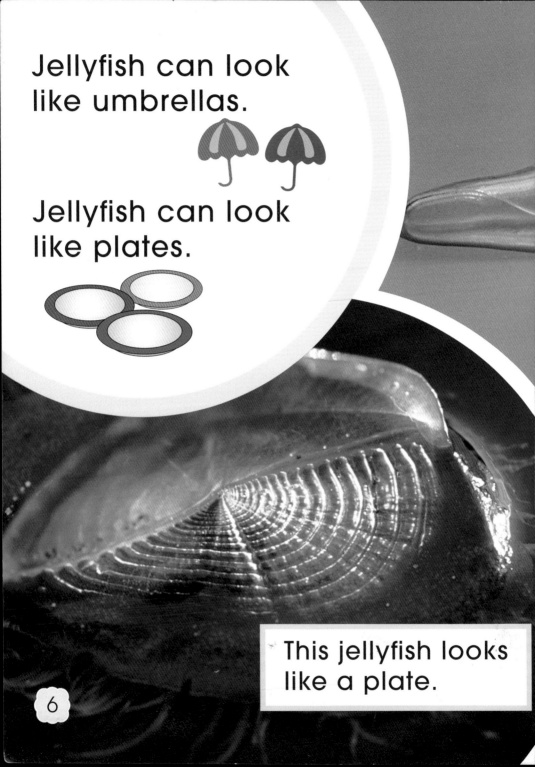

Jellyfish can look
like plates.

This jellyfish looks
like a plate.

This jellyfish looks like an umbrella.

7

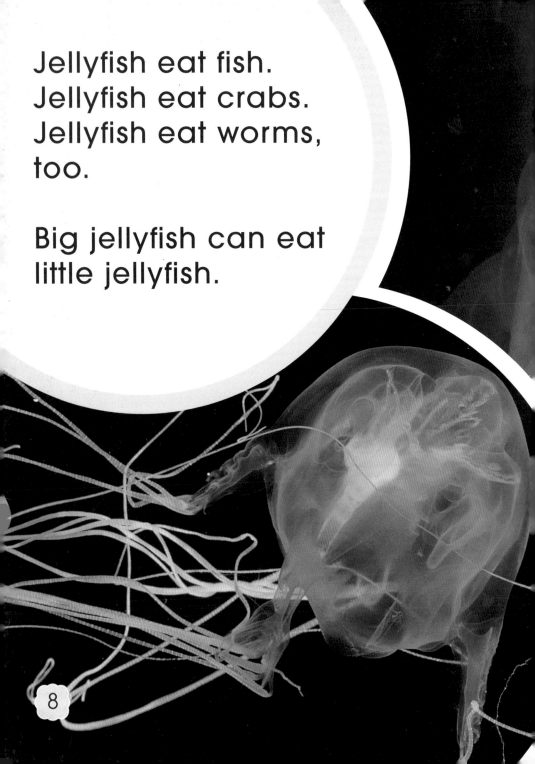

Jellyfish eat fish.
Jellyfish eat crabs.
Jellyfish eat worms,
too.

Big jellyfish can eat
little jellyfish.

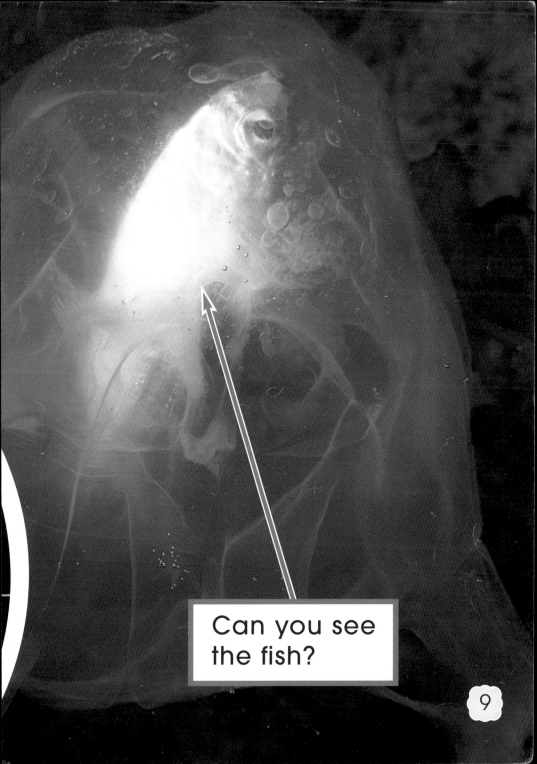

Can you see
the fish?

9

Look at the
tentacles.

The jellyfish can
get food with
its tentacles.

tentacles

11

Look at all
the jellyfish.

Jellyfish can float
in the water.

13

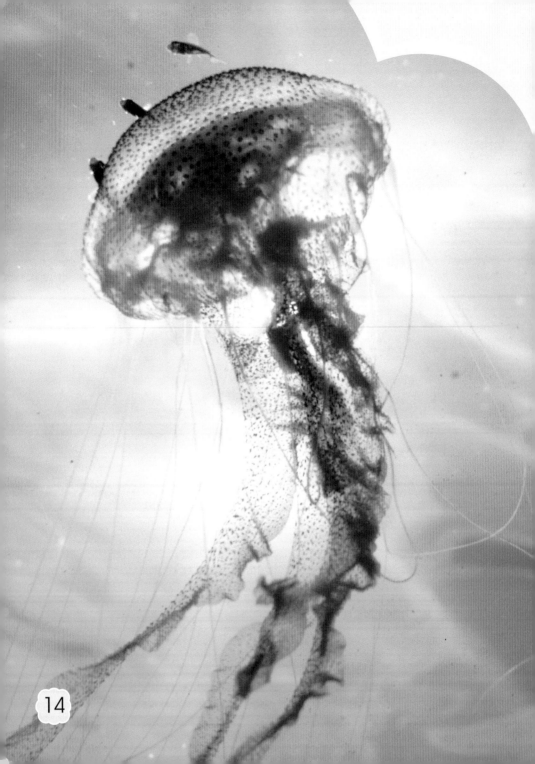

# Index

# Guide Notes

**Title: Jellyfish**

**Stage:** Early (2) – Yellow

**Genre:** Nonfiction (Expository)

**Approach:** Guided Reading

**Processes:** Thinking Critically, Exploring Language, Processing Information

**Written and Visual Focus:** Photographs (static images), Captions, Labels, Index

## THINKING CRITICALLY

(sample questions)

- What do you think this book is going to tell us?
- Look at the title and read it to the children.
- Ask the children what they know about jellyfish.
- Focus the children's attention on the Index. Ask: "What are you going to find out about in this book?"
- If you want to find out about tentacles, on which page would you look?
- Look at page 9. How do you think the jellyfish ate the fish?
- Look at pages 12 and 13. How do you think jellyfish can float in the water?

## EXPLORING LANGUAGE

### Terminology

Title, cover, photographs, author, photographers

### Vocabulary

**Interest words:** jellyfish, umbrellas, plates, crabs, worms, tentacles, float

**High-frequency words (reinforced):** look, this, at, it, is, can, get, be, the, too, a, you, little, big, like, its, in

**Compound word:** jellyfish

**Positional word:** in

### Print Conventions

Capital letter for sentence beginnings, periods, commas